Seeds of Sunshine

ISBN 978-1-68570-535-0 (paperback)
ISBN 978-1-68570-536-7 (digital)

Christian Faith Publishing
832 Park Avenue
Meadville, PA 16335
www.christianfaithpublishing.com

Printed in the United States of America

Seeds of Sunshine

Ellen Kolman

Every Tuesday after school, Sunshine visits his Grammy, and Grammy always has the yummiest snacks.

This Tuesday, Sunshine wasn't gobbling down his food in his usual enthusiastic way.

"Is there something bothering you, Sunshine?" Grammy asked after a few long moments of watching Sunshine pick at his honey and nuts with fresh blueberries.

"One of the kids said something that hurt my feelings today," Sunshine answered quietly after a heavy sigh.

"Come," said Grammy as she hung up her apron and pulled on her rubber boots. "Let's go for a nature walk on the path beyond the pond."

Sunshine put on his cap and took Grammy's hand, and together, they discovered some wonderful things. First, Grammy spied a cocoon.

"Oh, what a treasure this is," Grammy told Sunshine.

"It's empty. There's nothing in it," Sunshine said, frowning.

"How can it be a treasure?"

"It is very special because of the treasure that came out of it. A caterpillar attached itself to a tree limb and wove this cocoon around itself. After some time, the caterpillar began to change, and when the change was done, it started to push its way out." Grammy stopped and smiled at Sunshine's curious expression.

"Did it get out? What did it change into?" Sunshine asked.

"Yes, yes, it did," said Grammy. "It became a beautiful, colorful butterfly! And it's probably fluttering nearby right now."

Sunshine looked all around, and he saw several orange-and-black butterflies, floating near the wildflowers.

As Grammy and Sunshine continued their walk, Grammy talked about how the Bible says, "When anyone believes in Jesus, he is a new creature; old things are gone; now all things are new" (2 Corinthians 5:17 ESV).

"Just like the caterpillar in the cocoon," Grammy said, "we are changed when we accept Jesus's love and forgiveness. Before Jesus, we would say unkind words and be mean back to those who hurt our feelings. But as a new creature, we can love those around us, and that makes us beautiful like butterflies too."

"Hmmm, I don't know, Grammy. How can I love the kids at school who say mean things and hurt my feelings?" Sunshine asked, looking very sad.

"Look over here, Sunshine. What do you see across this field?"

"I see lots and lots of dandelion puffs! It looks like snow in summer," he said.

Grammy picked a handful of puffs and began to blow! As she blew, the seed puffs broke free from the stem and scattered on the breeze to all parts of the field.

Sunshine also picked some puffs, buried his nose in, and sniffed. "Achoo!" Sunshine sneezed, sending his puffs into the breeze. Giggling, he had fun watching the puffs float high in the air until they disappeared far away.

"The puffs are dandelion seeds," Grammy explained. "When the wind blows the puffs, it sends the seeds flying to new places so more dandelions will grow and bless us with their pretty yellow flowers. Our words are like the puffs. When we speak, our words spread seeds to those around us. Those seeds can grow pretty flowers of joy, happiness, peace, comfort, encouragement, and kindness. Or our words can spread seeds that grow ugly weeds of sadness, doubt, fear, anger, and hurt."

Still holding his bouquet of puffs, Sunshine looked hard at them. He took a deep breath and *blew* as hard as he could! Smiling, he hugged Grammy and said, "I want my words to spread seeds of love and grow pretty flowers!"

Grammy held Sunshine tight and whispered, "If we all use our words to spread seeds of kindness, then soon there will be no room for ugly weeds to grow. So tomorrow, if those kids still use their words to hurt your feelings, Jesus will help you to forgive them and stay kind, and that will make you happy too."

Sunshine smiled up at Grammy and suddenly remembered he was hungry.

"Grammy, do you have any more blueberries?"

And they giggled as they walked back to Grammy's house.

"Be kind to one another, tenderhearted, forgiving one another, as God in Christ forgave you" (Ephesians 4:32 ESV).

The end!

About the Author

Ellen Kolman has a passion for teaching children the love of Jesus. For more than thirty years, she has taught and entertained children in both church and Christian school settings. Currently, Ellen teaches kindergarten and first grade where the challenge of finding creative ways to help children understand kindness inspired her to write her first children's book, *Seeds of Sunshine*. Ellen, along with her husband, Andy, lives in Ashtabula, Ohio. They have five grown children and two grandchildren, who are the *sunshine* in their lives.

CPSIA information can be obtained
at www.ICGtesting.com
Printed in the USA
JSHW062008070123
35751JS00004B/38

9 781685 705350